THE NOISY WOODS

BY: KADE ROBERSON

ILLUSTRATIONS BY: MARIAH RUPP

SHHHH,
LISTEN, DO YOU HEAR THAT?

IS IT THE HUNGRY CHIPMUNK CHOMPING ON ACORNS?

NO THAT'S NOT IT
IT IS MUCH MUCH
LOUDER
THAN THAT.

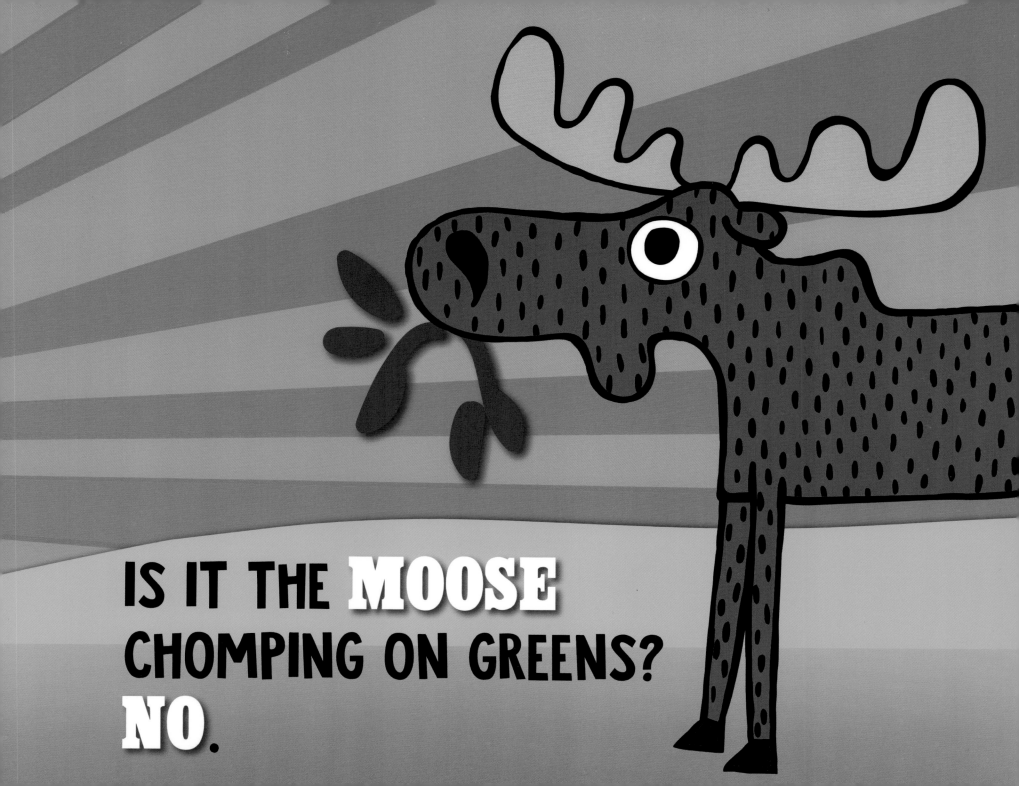

THE BEES **BUZZING** IN THE WILDFLOWERS?

THE
WOODPECKER
PECKING
AT TREES?

IS IT THE OWL,
HOOTING SOFTLY
HIGH IN IT'S NEST?
HOOT HOOT

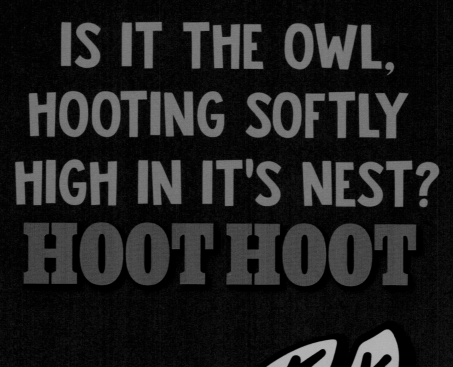

THE BEAR SNORING IN HIS DEN?

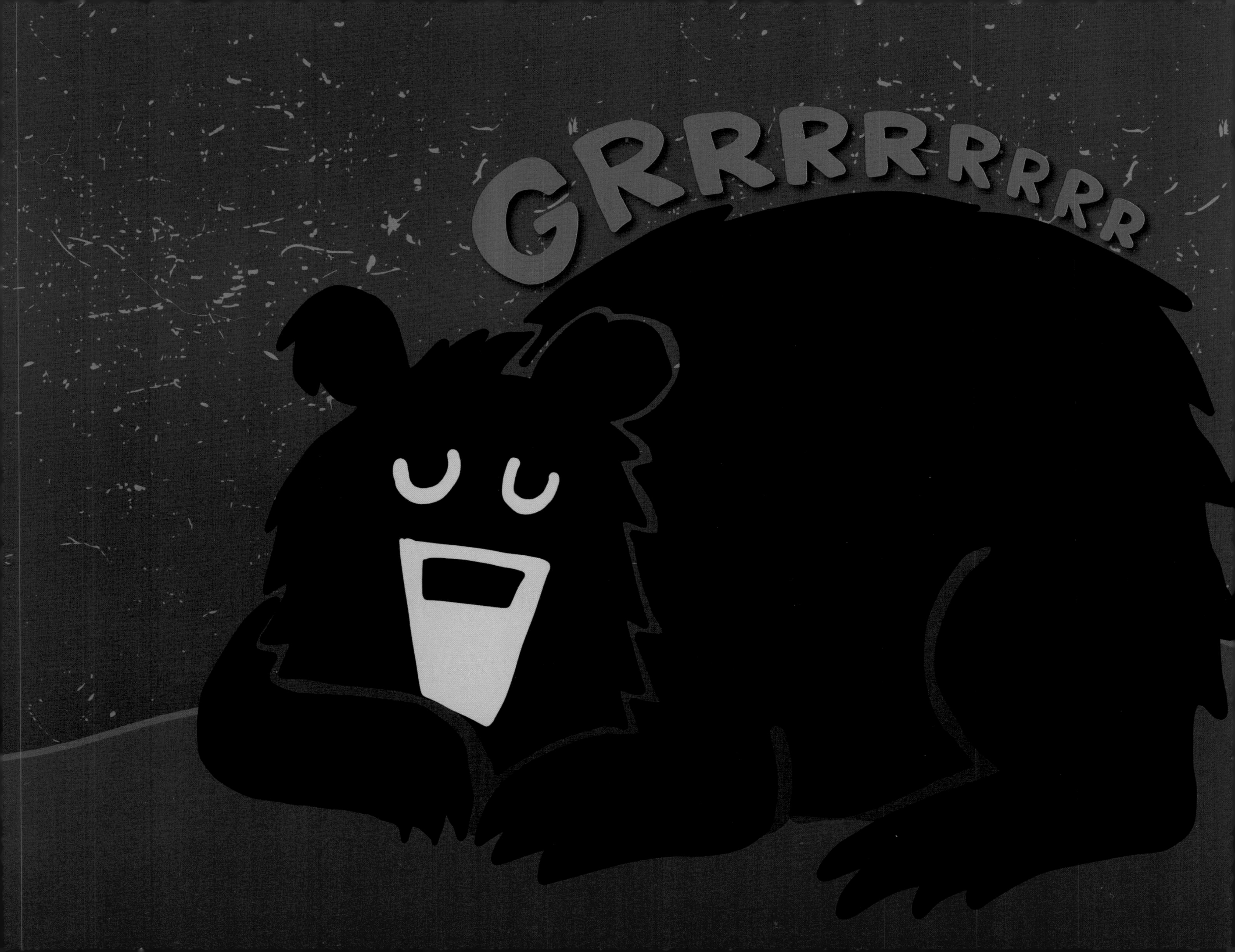
GRRRRRRRR

NOPE,
THOSE ARE ALL NOISY, BUT IT ISN'T ANY OF THOSE THINGS.

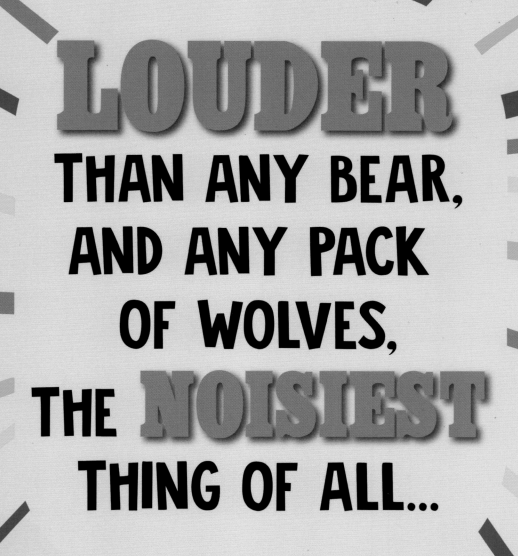